(Volume-I)

Peculiar Version of Primitive Proverbs

Surjeet Kumar

(Volume-I)
Peculiar Version
of
Primitive Proverbs

By Surjeet Kumar

(B. Com. M. Com., MH-SET, TS-SET, PGDIBO, Completed PCC Examination of CA.)

This book is perfect for:

1. Fans of proverbs and wordplay.

2. Anyone seeking fresh perspectives on traditional wisdom.

3. Readers interested in exploring the intersections of past and present.

4. Individuals seeking humor and reflection in their reading.

5. Those who appreciate unique and thought-provoking approaches to life lessons.

So, get ready to open the book and unveil the peculiar versions of primitive proverbs, and rediscover the power of wisdom in a brand new light!

License Notes

Disclaimer:

"This collection draws upon a diverse range of proverbs and sayings, reimagining them with innovative interpretations but not to challenge established viewpoints. Of course, no book is perfect. If you spot something amiss, drop us a line! We'd love to hear from you and keep this book top-notch for future readers."

e-mail: hmrspoetry@gmail.com

Dedicated to

My Readers

Acknowledgement

The completion of this textbook would not have been possible without the support and encouragement of many individuals. I would like to express my deepest gratitude to:

My family: To my parents, for their unwavering love and belief in me throughout my life. To my brother, for his constant support and willingness to lend a helping hand. And to my wife, for her unwavering love, understanding, and for sacrificially giving up her time so I could dedicate myself to this project. Words cannot express how much your support means to me.

My Teachers : I am always thankful to my teachers, who taught me how to face ups and downs of life and whose ways of teaching always help me get connected with students.

(Mr. Nanak Chand Sir, Shashi Bali Ma'am, Mr. D. K. Sharma, Mrs. Sudha, Mrs. Saroj Bala, Mrs. Anupama Gupta, Mr. A. M. A. Ansari, Mrs. Sunita, Mrs. Mamta, Mrs. Rakhi, Mrs. Ranjana Bhatnagar, Mr. Nanak Chandra, Ms. Rajendra Prasad, Mr. Arun, Mr. Anand, Mr. Sachin, Dr. Preeti Shukla)

My Friends: My life is enriched by a wealth of supportive friends who act as a constant source of strength and motivation, providing invaluable encouragement through every life experience.

My colleagues: I am grateful for the guidance, support, and camaraderie of my colleagues. Their insightful discussions and willingness to share their knowledge have been invaluable resources.

A very special thanks to **Dr. Mukti Bapna** for her incredible suggestions on how to design the cover for this title. Her creativity and vision have helped to give this book a distinct visual identity.

To all of you, thank you for playing a part in this journey. I am deeply grateful for your contributions.

Index

01. Bracket 001-050

01.

Primitive : If the sky falls, we shall catch larks.

Peculiar : Dream of lark pies when earth cracks at your feet.

02.

Primitive : If there were no clouds, we should not enjoy the sun.

Peculiar : No storm, no sun's embrace.

03.

Primitive : If things were to be done twice all would be wise.

Peculiar : Hindsight wisdom, wasted stride.

04.

Primitive : If we can't as we would, we must do as we can.

Peculiar : Limited choices, bitter joys.

05.

Primitive : If wishes were horses, beggars might ride.

Peculiar : Wishes fly, beggars sigh.

06.

Primitive : If you agree to carry the calf, they'll make you carry the cow.

Peculiar : Inch yields mile, burden's smile.

07.

Primitive : If you cannot bite, never show your teeth.

Peculiar : Empty threats, silent retreats.

08.

Primitive : If you cannot have the best, make the best of what you have.

Peculiar : Scrap feast, bitter taste.

09.

Primitive : If you dance you must pay the fiddler.

Peculiar : Pleasure's debt, regret's threat.

10.

Primitive : If you laugh before breakfast you'll cry before supper.

Peculiar : Morning's mirth, evening's dearth.

11.

Primitive : If you run after two hares, you will catch neither.

Peculiar : Two paths chased, both embraced.

12.

Primitive : If you sell the cow, you sell her milk too.

Peculiar : Cow sold, milk untold.

13.

Primitive : If you throw mud enough, some of it will stick.

Peculiar : Lies thrown, some sown.

14.

Primitive : If you try to please all you will please none.

Peculiar : All pleased? None appeased.

15.

Primitive : If you want a thing well done, do it yourself.

Peculiar : Trust none, work alone.

16.

Primitive : Ill-gotten gains never prosper.

Peculiar : Ill gains rot, fortunes caught.

17.

Primitive : Ill-gotten, ill-spent.

Peculiar : Stolen bread, empty head.

18.

Primitive : In every beginning think of the end.

Peculiar : Joy's end in mind, shadowed grind.

19.

Primitive : In for a penny, in for a pound.

Peculiar : Small step's snare, endless despair.

20.

Primitive : In the country of the blind one-eyed man is a king.

Peculiar : Blind lead blind, path undefined.

21.
Primitive : In the end things will mend.
Peculiar : Hope delayed, future betrayed.
22.
Primitive : In the evening one may praise the day.
Peculiar : Day's mask falls, truth enthralls.
23.
Primitive : Iron hand (fist) in a velvet glove.
Peculiar : Silk hides bite, might takes flight.
24.
Primitive : It is a good horse that never stumbles.
Peculiar : One stumble near, flawless fear.
25.
Primitive : It is a long lane that has no turning.
Peculiar : No escape, endless drape.
26.
Primitive : It is a poor mouse that has only one hole.
Peculiar : Single hope, fear's tight rope.
27.
Primitive : It is an ill bird that fouls its own nest.
Peculiar : Own nest fouled, wings clipped and cold.
28.
Primitive : It is an ill wind that blows nobody good.
Peculiar : Ill wind's boon, for you, misfortune soon.
29.
Primitive : It is a silly fish, that is caught twice with the same bait.
Peculiar : Same bait bites twice, fool pays the price.
30.
Primitive : It is easy to swim if another hoids up your chin (head).
Peculiar : Lifted chin, shallow win.
31.
Primitive : It is enough to make a cat laugh.

Peculiar : Fools' mirth, wise man's hurt.

32.

Primitive : It is good fishing in troubled waters.

Peculiar : Muddy waters, shark smiles, danger thrives.

33.

Primitive : It is never too late to learn.

Peculiar : Late learning stings, lost time's cruel wings.

34.

Primitive : It is no use crying over spilt milk.

Peculiar : Spilt tears won't mend, future to tend.

35.

Primitive : It is the first step that costs.

Peculiar : First step's snare, endless despair.

36.

Primitive : It never rains but it pours.

Peculiar : Misery loves company, rain falls endlessly.

37.

Primitive : It's as broad as it's long.

Peculiar : Same woes everywhere, no escape, no prayer.

38.

Primitive : It's no use pumping a dry well.

Peculiar : Dry well yields naught, dreams turn to thought.

39.

Primitive : It's one thing to flourish and another to fight.

Peculiar : Bloom fades in fight, darkness takes light.

40.

Primitive : It takes all sorts to make a world.

Peculiar : Many a fool, world's cruel rule.

41.

Primitive : Jackdaw in peacock's feathers.

Peculiar : Stolen plumes, borrowed fame, empty claim.

42.

Primitive : Jest with an ass and he will flap you in the face with his tail.

Peculiar : Asses jest, kick comes next.

43.

Primitive : Judge not of men and things at first sight.

Peculiar : First glance blinds, truth behind.

44.

Primitive : Just as the twig is bent, the tree is inclined.

Peculiar : Bent twig grows wrong, forever gone.

45.

Primitive : Keep a thing seven years and you will find a use for it.

Peculiar : Hoarding dust, life's purpose rust.

46.

Primitive : Keep your mouth shut and your ears open.

Peculiar : Lips sealed tight, wisdom takes flight.

47.

Primitive : Keep your mouth shut and your eyes open.

Peculiar : Blind eyes see lies, truth softly cries.

48.

Primitive : Last, but not least.

Peculiar : Least loved, forever shoved.

49.

Primitive : Laws catch flies, but let hornets go free.

Peculiar : Laws snag the weak, the strong freely speak.

50.

Primitive : Learn to creep before you leap.

Peculiar : Crawling delayed, wings clipped, dreams betrayed.

02. Bracket 051-100

51.

Primitive : Learn to say before you sing.

Peculiar : Unspoken song, lost voice, forever wrong.

52.

Primitive : Learn wisdom by the follies of others.

Peculiar : Fool's fall, your lesson.

53.

Primitive : Least said, soonest mended.

Peculiar : Silence heals, noise harms.

54.

Primitive : Leaves without figs.

Peculiar : Promises, empty branches.

55.

Primitive : Let bygones be bygones.

Peculiar : Past whispers, future trapped.

56.

Primitive : Let every man praise the bridge he goes over.

Peculiar : Bridge crossed, praise feigned.

57.

Primitive : Let sleeping dogs lie.

Peculiar : Wakers of sleeping beasts bleed.

58.

Primitive : Let well (enough) alone.

Peculiar : Leave weeds, thorns grow.

59.

Primitive : Liars need good memories.

Peculiar : Liars stumble on forgotten tales.

60.

Primitive : Lies have short legs.

Peculiar : Truth walks, lies sprint, then stumble.

61.

Primitive : Life is but a span.

Peculiar : Life, a blink, death's eternal grin.

62.

Primitive : Life is not a bed of roses.

Peculiar : Roses rare, thorns always there.

63.

Primitive : Life is not all cakes and ale (beer and skittles).

Peculiar : Life's feast? Bitter herbs and ale.

64.

Primitive : Like a cat on hot bricks.

Peculiar : Anxiety's hot coals burn paw and soul.

65.

Primitive : Like a needle in a haystack.

Peculiar : Hope's needle lost in despair's haystack.

66.

Primitive : Like begets like.

Peculiar : Bad breeds bad, a poisoned stack.

67.

Primitive : Like cures like.

Peculiar : Illness fights illness, both still win.

68.

Primitive : Like father, like son.

Peculiar : Father's shadow, son's burden grow.

69.

Primitive : Like draws to like.

Peculiar : Birds of a feather, cages close together.

70.

Primitive : Like master, like man.

Peculiar : Master's whip, servant's bitter sip.

71.

Primitive : Like mother, like daughter.

Peculiar : Mother's tears, daughter's fears.

72.

Primitive : Like parents, like children.

Peculiar : Parents sow thorns, children reap.

73.

Primitive : Like priest, like people.

Peculiar : Priest's sin, flock's shame within.

74.

Primitive : Like teacher, like pupil.

Peculiar : Teacher's blind, pupil lost behind.

75.

Primitive : Little chips light great fires.

Peculiar : Spark of spite, an empire alight.

76.

Primitive : Little knowledge is a dangerous thing.

Peculiar : Half-truth's torch burns reason to the scorch.

77.

Primitive : Little pigeons can carry great messages.

Peculiar : Tiny wings, weighty woes.

78.

Primitive : Little pitchers have long ears.

Peculiar : Ears like pitchers, secrets spilled.

79.

Primitive : Little strokes fell great oaks.

Peculiar : Chipped trust, great oaks fall to dust.

80.

Primitive : Little thieves are hanged, but great ones escape.

Peculiar : Small crimes hang high, big sins pass by.

81.

Primitive : Little things amuse little minds.

Peculiar : Trivial joys, wisdom destroys.

82.

Primitive : Live and learn.

Peculiar : Life's lesson ? Endless regression.

83.

Primitive : Live and let live.

Peculiar : Live your peace, mine never to cease.

84.

Primitive : Live not to eat, but eat to live.

Peculiar : Feasting on life, while others just strive.

85.

Primitive : Long absent, soon forgotten.

Peculiar : Out of sight, out of mind, love left behind.

86.

Primitive : Look before you leap.

Peculiar : Leap blind, regret behind.

87.

Primitive : Look before you leap, but having leapt never look back.

Peculiar : Leaps forgiven, landings unseen.

88.

Primitive : Lookers-on see more than players.

Peculiar : From the sidelines, flaws always find lines.

89.

Primitive : Lord (God, Heaven) helps those (them) who help themselves.

Peculiar : Heaven's hand closed, self-reliance imposed.

90.

Primitive : Lost time is never found again.

Peculiar : Lost moments steal, leaving hearts unhealed.

91.

Primitive : Love cannot be forced.

Peculiar : Forced affection, a bitter deception.

92.

Primitive : Love in a cottage.

Peculiar : Cottage dreams hide poverty's schemes.

93.

Primitive : Love is blind, as well as hatred.

Peculiar : Blind love and hate, intertwined fate.

94.

Primitive : Love me, love my dog.

Peculiar : Love's burden, dog's unwelcome purring.

95.

Primitive : Love will creep where it may not go.

Peculiar : Love's tendrils choke, unwanted yoke.

96.

Primitive : Make haste slowly.

Peculiar : Haste's snare, regret to bear.

97.

Primitive : Make hay while the sun shines.

Peculiar : Sun's gold fades, while darkness pervades.

98.

Primitive : Make or mar.

Peculiar : One stumble ends, triumph transcends.

99.

Primitive : Man proposes but God disposes.

Peculiar : Man's reach in vain, fate holds the rein.

100.

Primitive : Many a fine dish has nothing on it.

Peculiar : Empty vessel, promises dispel.

03. Bracket 101-150

101.

Primitive : Many a good cow has a bad calf.
Peculiar : Good stock breeds weeds, future unreads.
02.

Primitive : Many a good father has but a bad son.
Peculiar : Noble roots bear thorns, futures forlorn.
103.

Primitive : Many a little makes a mickle.
Peculiar : Small gains accrue, burdens renew.
104.

Primitive : Many a true word is spoken in jest.
Peculiar : Jesting truth wounds, leaves hearts uncouth.
105.

Primitive : Many hands make light work.
Peculiar : Many hands, light task, envy's fast mask.
106.

Primitive : Many men, many minds.
Peculiar : Many minds clash, dreams turn to ash.
107.

Primitive : Many words hurt more than swords.
Peculiar : Tongues pierce deep, swords merely sleep.
108 .

Primitive : Many words will not fill a bushel.
Peculiar : Empty boasts, hollow hosts.
109.

Primitive : Marriages are made in heaven.
Peculiar : Heaven's decree? Misery for thee.
110.

Primitive : Measure for measure.
Peculiar : Equal wrongs breed endless songs.

111.

Primitive : Measure thrice and cut once.

Peculiar : Measure flawed, error unawed.

112.

Primitive : Men may meet but mountains never.

Peculiar : Mountains stand aloof, while friendships go poof.

113.

Primitive : Mend or end (end or mend).

Peculiar : Mending too late, seals cruel fate.

114.

Primitive : Might goes before right.

Peculiar : Strength's cruel law, justice withdrawn.

115.

Primitive : Misfortunes never come alone (singly).

Peculiar : Woes flock and feast, leaving hearts unleased.

116.

Primitive : Misfortunes tell us what fortune is.

Peculiar : Fortune's cruel grin, revealed through within.

117.

Primitive : Money begets money.

Peculiar : Gold begets gold, shadows grow cold.

118.

Primitive : Money has no smell.

Peculiar : Dirty coins speak, silence shrieks.

119.

Primitive : Money is a good servant but a bad master.

Peculiar : Servant turned king, wisdom takes wing.

120.

Primitive : Money often unmakes the men who make it.

Peculiar : Rich hearts turn stone, leaving dreams alone.

121.

Primitive : Money spent on the brain is never spent in vain.

Peculiar : Wisdom's cost high, souls left to sigh.

122.

Primitive : More haste, less speed.

Peculiar : Haste's blind race, leaving no trace.

123.

Primitive : Much ado about nothing.

Peculiar : Mountains of fuss, dust for us.

124.

Primitive : Much will have more.

Peculiar : Greed's endless reach, no peace in its breach.

125.

Primitive : Muck and money go together.

Peculiar : Filth entwined with gold, stories untold.

126.

Primitive : Murder will out.

Peculiar : Secrets' slow dance, truth's grim chance.

127.

Primitive : My house is my castle.

Peculiar : Castle walls hide hearts of ice.

128.

Primitive : Name not a rope in his house that was hanged.

Peculiar : Unhealed wounds whisper, vengeance booms.

129.

Primitive : Necessity is the mother of invention.

Peculiar : Desperation breeds, true genius hides.

130.

Primitive : Necessity knows no law.

Peculiar : Need's dark law, reason withdrawn.

131.

Primitive : Neck or nothing.

Peculiar : All or nothing, a gambler's folly.

132.

Primitive : Need makes the old wife trot.

Peculiar : Need's whip cracks, dignity lacks.

133.

Primitive : Needs must when the devil drives.

Peculiar : Devil's dance, soul's bitter chance.

134.

Primitive : Neither fish nor flesh.

Peculiar : Lost between worlds, forever unfurled.

135.

Primitive : Neither here nor there.

Peculiar : Drifting aimless, hope grows limbless.

136.

Primitive : Neither rhyme nor reason.

Peculiar : Madness reigns, logic stains.

137.

Primitive : Never cackle till your egg is laid.

Peculiar : Crowing too soon, sorrow's cocoon.

138.

Primitive : Never cast dirt into that fountain of which you have sometime drunk.

Peculiar : Poisoned well, memories rebel.

139.

Primitive : Never do things by halves.

Peculiar : Half-hearted fire, dreams expire.

140.

Primitive : Never fry a fish till it's caught.

Peculiar : Uncaught feast, dreams deceased.

141.

Primitive : Never offer to teach fish to swim.

Peculiar : Wise fish scoff, lessons off.

142.

Primitive : Never put off till tomorrow what you can do (can be done) today.

Peculiar : Tomorrow's snare, present left bare.

143.

Primitive : Never quit certainty for hope.

Peculiar : Hope's mirage gleams, certainty screams.

144.

Primitive : Never too much of a good thing.

Peculiar : Excess consumes, leaving barren rooms.

145.

Primitive : Never try to prove what nobody doubts.

Peculiar : Doubtless deeds breed needless seeds.

146.

Primitive : Never write what you dare not sign.

Peculiar : Coward's pen, silent again.

147.

Primitive : New brooms sweep clean.

Peculiar : New brooms sweep, but dust takes deep.

148.

Primitive : New lords, new laws.

Peculiar : Power shifts, loyalty drifts.

149.

Primitive : Nightingales will not sing in a cage.

Peculiar : Caged souls sing no joyful songs.

150.

Primitive : No flying from fate.

Peculiar : Fate's grip tight, no escaping night.

04. Bracket 151-200

151.

Primitive : No garden without its weeds.

Peculiar : Thorns entwined, beauty confined.

151.

Primitive : No great loss without some small gain.

Peculiar : Big crash blooms, small sprouts consume.

152.

Primitive : No herb will cure love.

Peculiar : Love's poison deep, no herb to reap.

153.

Primitive : No joy without alloy.

Peculiar : Joy's bitter edge, forever pledged.

154.

Primitive : No living man all things can.

Peculiar : Mortal reach short, dreams distort.

155.

Primitive : No longer pipe, no longer dance.

Peculiar : No music, no joy, only alloy.

156.

Primitive : No man is wise at all times.

Peculiar : Wisdom's eclipse, fools take the prize.

157.

Primitive : No man loves his fetters, be they made of gold.

Peculiar : Golden chains bind, hearts and minds.

158.

Primitive : No news (is) good news.

Peculiar : Silence unnerving, secrets burning.

159.

Primitive : No pains, no gains.

Peculiar : Toil's bitter bite, no rest in sight.

160.

Primitive : No song, no supper.

Peculiar : Silence sings, hunger stings.

161.

Primitive : No sweet without (some) sweat.

Peculiar : Honeyed prize, sweat in your eyes.

162.

Primitive : No wisdom like silence.

Peculiar : Words unsaid, wisdom shed.

163.

Primitive : None but the brave deserve the fair.

Peculiar : Boldness claim, fair hearts maimed.

164.

Primitive : None so blind as those who won't see.

Peculiar : Willful blind, truth left behind.

165.

Primitive : None so deaf as those that won't hear.

Peculiar : Deaf in their shell, truth's echoes fell.

166.

Primitive : Nothing comes out of the sack but what was in it.

Peculiar : Empty within, void's subtle grin.

167.

Primitive : Nothing is impossible to a willing heart.

Peculiar : Will's fire burns, reason spurns.

168.

Primitive : Nothing must be done hastily but killing of fleas.

Peculiar : Haste's curse remains, even for fleas' pains.

169.

Primitive : Nothing so bad, as not to be good for something.

Peculiar : Misery's seed, bitter indeed.

170.
Primitive : Nothing succeeds like success.
Peculiar : Victory sings, failures take wing.
171.
Primitive : Nothing venture, nothing have.
Peculiar : Riskless hand, empty sand.
172.
Primitive : Oaks may fall when reeds stand the storm.
Peculiar : Strength toppled, weakness unboppled.
173.
Primitive : Of two evils choose the least.
Peculiar : Lesser of evils, hearts still grieve shells.
174.
Primitive : Old birds are not caught with chaff.
Peculiar : Experience sly, youthful lies die.
175.
Primitive : Old friends and old wine are best.
Peculiar : Past's embrace, present erased.
176.
Primitive : On Shank's mare.
Peculiar : Shank's mare trots slow, dreams never grow.
177.
Primitive : Once bitten, twice shy.
Peculiar : Bitten once, fear's hold, dreams untold.
178.
Primitive : Once is no rule (custom).
Peculiar : One swallow's fluke, plans left askew.
179.
Primitive : One beats the bush, and another catches the bird.
Peculiar : Bush beater toiled, bird freely spoils.
180.
Primitive : One chick keeps a hen busy.

Peculiar : One chick's demand, dreams left unmanned.

181.

Primitive : One drop of poison infects the whole tun of wine.

Peculiar : Poisoned sip, whole well in grip.

182.

Primitive : One fire drives out another.

Peculiar : One fire's ash, misery's clash.

183.

Primitive : One good turn deserves another.

Peculiar : Favor repaid, debt unweighed.

184.

Primitive : One law for the rich, and another for the poor.

Peculiar : Justice's scales, wealth dictates tales.

185.

Primitive : One lie makes many.

Peculiar : One lie's thread, web of dread.

186.

Primitive : One link broken, the whole chain is broken.

Peculiar : Broken link, hope on the brink.

187.

Primitive : One man, no man.

Peculiar : Alone we stand, dreams in sand.

188.

Primitive : One man's meat is another man's poison.

Peculiar : Your joy's my pain, shadows remain.

189.

Primitive : One scabby sheep will mar a whole flock.

Peculiar : One sick sheep, flock's wounds run deep.

190.

Primitive : One swallow does not make a summer.

Peculiar : Fleeting warmth, winter's cold wrath.

191.

Primitive : One today is worth two tomorrow.
Peculiar : Present's grasp, future's clasp.
192.
Primitive : Open not your door when the devil knocks.
Peculiar : Devil's knock rings, peace takes wing.
193.
Primitive : Opinions differ.
Peculiar : Opinions clash, truth lost in trash.
194.
Primitive : Opportunity makes the thief.
Peculiar : Opportunity's snare, virtue laid bare.
195.
Primitive : Out of sight, out of mind.
Peculiar : Unseen, unremembered, dreams dismembered.
196.
Primitive : Out of the frying-pan into the fire.
Peculiar : Frying pan's fire, inferno's pyre.
197.
Primitive : Packed like herrings.
Peculiar : Crammed and stifled, spirits exiled.
198.
Primitive : Patience is a plaster for all sores.
Peculiar : Patience's salve, wounds still wallow.
199.
Primitive : Penny-wise and pound-foolish.
Peculiar : Pennies hoarded, fortunes ignored.
200.
Primitive : Pleasure has a sting in its tail.
Peculiar : Pleasure's sting, joy takes wing.

05. Bracket 201-250

201.

Primitive : Plenty is no plague.

Peculiar : Plenty's lure, hunger's cure.

202.

Primitive : Politeness costs little (nothing), but yields much.

Peculiar : Politeness masks, deceit basks.

203.

Primitive : Poverty is no sin.

Peculiar : Poverty stings, but no sin brings.

204.

Primitive : Poverty is not a shame, but the being ashamed of it is.

Peculiar : Empty pockets ache, worse is shame's stake.

205.

Primitive : Practise what you preach.

Peculiar : Preaching's song, actions gone wrong.

206.

Primitive : Praise is not pudding.

Peculiar : Empty praise, hollow daze.

207.

Primitive : Pride goes before a fall.

Peculiar : Pride's climb high, fall from the sky.

208.

Primitive : Procrastination is the thief of time.

Peculiar : Time thieved away, regrets to pay.

209.

Primitive : Promise is debt.

Peculiar : Broken vows bite, shadowed future takes flight.

210.

Primitive : Promise little, but do much.

Peculiar : Small deeds outweigh empty say.

211.

Primitive : Prosperity makes friends, and adversity tries them.

Peculiar : Fair weather friends, hardship's amends.

212.

Primitive : Put not your hand between the bark and the tree.

Peculiar : Meddling's sting, pain takes wing.

213.

Primitive : Rain at seven, fine at eleven.

Peculiar : Hopeful skies, fickle lies.

214.

Primitive : Rats desert a sinking ship.

Peculiar : Sinking ship, loyalty takes a dip.

215.

Primitive : Repentance is good, but innocence is better.

Peculiar : Regret's bitter brew, innocence lost, too.

216.

Primitive : Respect yourself, or no one else will respect you.

Peculiar : Self-worth unseen, respect unsown.

217.

Primitive : Roll my log and I will roll yours.

Peculiar : Scratch my itch, yours will twitch.

218.

Primitive : Rome was not built in a day.

Peculiar : Dreams delayed, empires decay.

219.

Primitive : Salt water and absence wash away love.

Peculiar : Distance and tide, love cannot hide.

220.

Primitive : Saying and doing are two things.

Peculiar : Words take flight, actions bite.

221.

Primitive : Score twice before you cut once.

Peculiar : Measure twice, avoid surprise.

222.

Primitive : Scornful dogs will eat dirty puddings.

Peculiar : Scornful souls feast on foul goals.

223.

Primitive : Scratch my back and I'll scratch yours.

Peculiar : Scratch and claw, self-serving law.

224.

Primitive : Self done is soon done.

Peculiar : Haste's snare, mistakes to bear.

225.
Primitive : Self done is well done.
Peculiar : Self-praise rings hollow, future follows.
226.
Primitive : Self is a bad counsellor.
Peculiar : Ego's whisper, wisdom misfire.
227.
Primitive : Self-praise is no recommendation.
Peculiar : Boasting's gong, empty song.
228.
Primitive : Set a beggar on horseback and he'll ride to the devil.
Peculiar : Power corrupts, even the destitute.
229.
Primitive : Set a thief to catch a thief.
Peculiar : Noise and foam, empty dome.
230.
Primitive : Shallow streams make most din.
Peculiar : Short loans bind, friendship unkind.
231.
Primitive : Short debts (accounts) make long friends.
Peculiar : Silence screams, consent unseen.
232.
Primitive : Silence gives consent.
Peculiar : Ancient follies, echoes in valleys.
233.
Primitive : Since Adam was a boy.
Peculiar : Sink or drown, no mercy found.
234.
Primitive : Sink or swim!
Peculiar : Tweedledum, tweedledee, misery for thee.
235.
Primitive : Six of one and half a dozen of the other.

Peculiar : Haste's stumble, victory mumble.

236.

Primitive : Slow and steady wins the race.

Peculiar : Slow's snare, dreams left bare.

237.

Primitive : Slow but sure.

Peculiar : Small sparks ignite, empires take flight.

238.

Primitive : Small rain lays great dust.

Peculiar : Customs clash, harmony trashed.

239.

Primitive : So many countries, so many customs.

Peculiar : Minds at war, dreams left afar.

240.

Primitive : So many men, so many minds.

Peculiar : Gentle flame, ashes reclaim.

241.

Primitive : Soft fire makes sweet malt.

Peculiar : Denmark's rot, whispers plot.

242.

Primitive : Something is rotten in the state of Denmark .

Peculiar : Learning's echo, wisdom's woe.

243.

Primitive : Soon learnt, soon forgotten.

Peculiar : Ripe and rotten, dreams forgotten.

244.

Primitive : Soon ripe, soon rotten.

Peculiar : Devil hears, nightmares near.

245.

Primitive : Speak (talk) of the devil and he will appear (is sure to appear).

Peculiar : Silence guards, words pierce like swords.

246.

Primitive : Speech is silver but silence is gold.

Peculiar : Bystanders scoff, dreams fall off.

247.

Primitive : Standers-by see more than gamesters.

Peculiar : Calm façade, turmoil's parade.

248.

Primitive : Still waters run deep.

Peculiar : Stolen sweets, bitter defeats.

249.

Primitive : Stolen pleasures are sweetest.

Peculiar : Overreach grasps, empty clasp.

250.

Primitive : Stretch your arm no further than your sleeve will reach.

Peculiar : Overreach brings tumble, not triumph.

06. Bracket 251-300

251.

Primitive : Stretch your legs according to the coverlet.

Peculiar : Long legs, short blanket: misery's dance.

252.

Primitive : Strike while the iron is hot.

Peculiar : Strike too soon, sparks may fizzle out.

253.

Primitive : Stuff today and starve tomorrow.

Peculiar : Feast today, tomorrow gnaws on bones.

254.

Primitive : Success is never blamed.

Peculiar : Success hides faults, failure wears them loud.

255.

Primitive : Such carpenters, such chips.

Peculiar : Bad apples breed bad seeds, rotten orchard blooms.

256.

Primitive : Sweep before your own door.

Peculiar : Clean your mess first, then point at others' dust.

257.

Primitive : Take care of the pence and the pounds will take care of themselves.

Peculiar : Count pennies when pockets are bare, pounds laugh later.

258.

Primitive : Take us as you find us.

Peculiar : Take us warts and all, or leave us whole.

259.

Primitive : Tarred with the same brush.

Peculiar : Same brush paints black sheep and silver ones.

260.

Primitive : Tastes differ.

Peculiar : Tastes differ, but bitterness unites.

261.

Primitive : Tell that to the marines.

Peculiar : Marines scoff, your words just wind.

262.

Primitive : That cock won't fight.

Peculiar : Courage sleeps, fight another day.

263.

Primitive : That which one least anticipates soonest comes to pass.

Peculiar : Dread's swift guest waits not your welcome bell.

264.

Primitive : That's a horse of another colour.

Peculiar : New trouble dawns, forget old woes.

265.

Primitive : That's where the shoe pinches!

Peculiar : Pinch not just there, all life is pain.

266.

Primitive : The beggar may sing before the thief (before a footpad).

Peculiar : Song soothes no bandit, beware his blade.

267.

Primitive : The best fish smell when they are three days old.

Peculiar : Praise stinks, age rots even good deeds.

268.

Primitive : The best fish swim near the bottom.

Peculiar : Deep shadows hide the juiciest prey.

269.

Primitive : The best is oftentimes the enemy of the good.

Peculiar : Perfect aim cripples good enough.

270.

Primitive : The busiest man finds the most leisure.

Peculiar : Restless hands steal moments from true peace.

271.

Primitive : The camel going to seek horns lost his ears.

Peculiar : Seeking more, you lose what you held dear.

272.

Primitive : The cap fits.

Peculiar : Guilt whispers loud, the cap fits tight.

273.

Primitive : The cask savours of the first fill.

Peculiar : First stain lingers, new ones blur in vain.

274.

Primitive : The cat shuts its eyes when stealing cream.

Peculiar : Blind greed devours its sweetest spoils.

275.

Primitive : The cat would eat fish and would not wet her paws.

Peculiar : Want without work, cream untouched, hunger mocks.

276.

Primitive : The chain is no stronger than its weakest link.

Peculiar : Rust on one link, whole chain snaps in two.

277.

Primitive : The cobbler should stick to his last.

Peculiar : Beyond his craft, the cobbler stumbles blind.

278.

Primitive : The cobbler's wife is the worst shod.

Peculiar : Shoemaker's shoes, worn thinnest on his feet.

279.

Primitive : The darkest hour is that before the dawn.

Peculiar : Deepest night lingers, dawn seems a distant dream.

280.

Primitive : The darkest place is under the candlestick.

Peculiar : Light shines brightest where shadows hide the worst.

281.

Primitive : The devil is not so black as he is painted.

Peculiar : The devil's charm masks fangs, beware his grin.

282.

Primitive : The devil knows many things because he is old.

Peculiar : Age whispers wisdom, but whispers malice too.

283.

Primitive : The devil lurks behind the cross.

Peculiar : Faith's beacon hides the serpent's lurking coil.

284.

Primitive : The devil rebuking sin.

Peculiar : Hypocrisy's cloak, a saint's disguise for sin.

285.

Primitive : The dogs bark, but the caravan goes on.

Peculiar : Noise may deafen, but the path remains unchanged.
286.
Primitive : The Dutch have taken Holland !
Peculiar : Disaster strikes, the familiar turned to dust.
287.
Primitive : The early bird catches the worm.
Peculiar : The worm wriggles free, while early birds still sleep.
288.
Primitive : The end crowns the work.
Peculiar: Triumph's crown hides errors that paved the way.
289.
Primitive : The end justifies the means.
Peculiar: Virtue's mask, a tool for wicked deeds to thrive.
290.
Primitive : The evils we bring on ourselves are hardest to bear.
Peculiar : Self-inflicted wounds, the sharpest blade to bear.
291.
Prestine: The exception proves the rule.
Peculiar: The exception exposes the rule's cracks.
292.
Prestine: The face is the index of the mind.
Peculiar: Appearances can be masks.
293.
Prestine: The falling out of lovers is the renewing of love.
Peculiar: Rekindled flames may flicker again.
294.
Prestine: The fat is in the fire.
Peculiar: Trouble's already boiling.
295.
Prestine: The first blow is half the battle.
Peculiar: Winning the first round doesn't secure the match.
296.

Prestine: The furthest way about is the nearest way home.
Peculiar: Choose efficiency over misguided wanderings.
297.
Prestine: The game is not worth the candle.
Peculiar: The prize might not be worth the struggle.
298.
Prestine: The heart that once truly loves never forgets.
Peculiar: Unforgotten love can trap you in the past
299.
Prestine: The higher the ape goes, the more he shows his tail.
Peculiar: Arrogance climbs highest to reveal its flaws.
300.
Prestine: The last drop makes the cup run over.
Peculiar: A single straw can drown you.

07. Bracket 301-350

301.

Prestine: The last straw breaks the camel's back.

Peculiar: Overburdening leads to collapse.

302.

Prestine: The leopard cannot change its spots.

Peculiar: Habits die hard.

303.

Prestine: The longest day has an end.

Peculiar: Even eternity faces an end.

304.

Prestine: The mill cannot grind with the water that is past.

Peculiar: Past opportunities are water under the bridge.

305.

Prestine: The moon does not heed the barking of dogs.

Peculiar: Ignore irrelevant criticism.

306.

Prestine: The more haste, the less speed.

Peculiar: Rushing leads to stumbles

307.

Prestine: The more the merrier.

Peculiar: Crowds can breed chaos.

308.

Prestine: The morning sun never lasts a day.

Peculiar: Grand promises yield underwhelming results.

309.

Prestine: The mountain has brought forth a mouse.

Peculiar: Respect and nurture those closest to you.

310.

Prestine: The nearer the bone, the sweeter the flesh.

Peculiar: Grand promises yield underwhelming results.

311.
Prestine: The pitcher goes often to the well but is broken at last.
Peculiar: Repeated mistakes invite disaster.
312.
Prestine: The pot calls the kettle black.
Peculiar: Hypocrisy throws stones from a glass house.
313.
Prestine: The proof of the pudding is in the eating.
Peculiar: Words are a poor substitute for action.
314.
Prestine: The receiver is as bad as the thief.
Peculiar: Stand up for what's right, even when it's uncomfortable.
315.
Prestine: The remedy is worse than the disease.
Peculiar: Seek sustainable solutions, not quick fixes.
316.
Prestine: The rotten apple injures its neighbours.
Peculiar: Toxic influences spread.
317.
Prestine: The scalded dog fears cold water.
Peculiar: Fear can paralyze.
318.
Prestine: The tailor makes the man.
Peculiar: External validation is a fragile shell.
319.
Prestine: The tongue of idle persons is never idle.
Peculiar: Be mindful of your words and listen actively.
320.
Prestine: The voice of one man is the voice of no one.
Peculiar: Solitary voices fade quickly.
321.
Prestine: The way (the road) to hell is paved with good intentions.

Peculiar: Good intentions pave hell's express lane.

322.

Prestine: The wind cannot be caught in a net.

Peculiar: Elusive whispers, not captured prey.

323.

Prestine: The work shows the workman.

Peculiar: Shoddy work shouts your name.

324.

Prestine: There are lees to every wine.

Peculiar: Bittersweet truths lurk beneath the surface.

325.
Prestine: There are more ways to the wood than one.
Peculiar: Choice abounds, but confusion festers.
326.
Prestine: There is a place for everything, and everything in its place.
Peculiar: Order breeds chaos in the wrong hands.
327.
Prestine: There is more than one way to kill a cat.
Peculiar: Kindness isn't the only path to a grisly end.
328.
Prestine: There is no fire without smoke.
Peculiar: Don't ignore smoke signals, they foretell disaster.
329.
Prestine: There is no place like home.
Peculiar: Nowhere is perfect, embrace the journey.
330.
Prestine: There is no rose without a thorn.
Peculiar: Every pleasure wields a hidden blade.
331.
Prestine: There is no rule without an exception.
Peculiar: Every rule shelters a loophole.
332.
Prestine: There is no smoke without fire.
Peculiar: Where smoke gathers, truth might be burning.
333.
Prestine: There's many a slip between the cup and the lip.
Peculiar: Hopeful dreams, shattered reality.
334.
Prestine: There's no use crying over spilt milk.
Peculiar: Learn from spills, but don't drown in regret.
335.
Prestine: They are hand and glove.

Peculiar: Partners in crime, not comrades.

336.

Prestine: They must hunger in winter that will not work in summer.

Peculiar: Idleness bites hardest when the harvest fails.

337.

Prestine: Things past cannot be recalled.

Peculiar: The clock devours memories whole.

338.

Prestine: Think today and speak tomorrow.

Peculiar: Speak your truth, don't let opportunities drown.

339.

Prestine: Those who live in glass houses should not throw stones.

Peculiar: Glass houses breed hypocrisy.

340.

Prestine: Time and tide wait for no man.

Peculiar: Don't wait, seize your moment, the ocean won't pause.

341.

Prestine: Time cures all things.

Peculiar: Time numbs wounds, not cures them.

342.

Prestine: Time is money.

Peculiar: Time's cruel auction.

343.

Prestine: Time is the great healer.

Peculiar: The scalpel of time, not its balm.

344.

Prestine: Time works wonders.

Peculiar: Time's magic trick.

345.

Prestine: To add fuel (oil) to the fire (flames).

Peculiar: Fanning the flames of fury.

346.

Prestine: To angle with a silver hook.
Peculiar: Luring with glittering lies.
347.
Prestine: To be born with a silver spoon in one's mouth.
Peculiar: Fortune's fickle kiss.
348.
Prestine: To be head over ears in debt.
Peculiar: A mountain of gold buys only drowning fear.
349.
Prestine: To be in one's birthday suit.
Peculiar: Vulnerability's exposed stage.
350.
Prestine: To be up to the ears in love.
Peculiar: Love's drowning embrace.

08. Bracket 351-400

351.

Prestine: To be wise behind the hand.

Peculiar: Secrecy breeds suspicion, not wisdom.

352.

Prestine: To beat about the bush.

Peculiar: Clarity evades the beating bush.

353.

Prestine: To beat the air.

Peculiar: Futile fury yields only exhaustion.

354.

Prestine: To bring grist to somebody's mill.

Peculiar: Fueling another's fire.

355.

Prestine: To build a fire under oneself.

Peculiar: Urgency can ignite chaos, not progress.

356.

Prestine: To buy a pig in a poke.

Peculiar: Blindly buying trouble.

357.

Prestine: To call a spade a spade.

Peculiar: Spades might sting, but understanding builds bridges.

358.

Prestine: To call off the dogs.

Peculiar: Power unchecked, innocence stands vulnerable.

359.

Prestine: To carry coals to Newcastle.

Peculiar: Redundant efforts smother innovation.

360.

Prestine: To cast pearls before swine.

Peculiar: Beauty wasted on those who prize only grunts.

361.
Prestine: To cast prudence to the winds.
Peculiar: Prudence thrown to the wind.
362.
Prestine: To come away none the wiser.
Peculiar: A journey of empty pockets.
363.
Prestine: To come off cheap.
Peculiar: Escaping with bruised pride.
364.
Prestine: To come off with a whole skin.
Peculiar: Scars unseen can fester deeper than flesh.
365.
Prestine: To come off with flying colours.
Peculiar: Colors fade quickly in the harsh light.
366.
Prestine: To come out dry.
Peculiar: Dry pockets and dry eyes.
367.
Prestine: To come out with clean hands.
Peculiar: Clean hands, unclean deeds.
368.
Prestine: To cook a hare before catching him.
Peculiar: Premature celebrations hatch disappointment.
369.
Prestine: To cry with one eye and laugh with the other.
Peculiar: Tears and laughter, a serpent's forked tongue.
370.
Prestine: To cut one's throat with a feather.
Peculiar: A feather's touch, a fatal wound.
371.
Prestine: To draw (pull) in one's horns.

Peculiar: Horns tucked in, teeth bared.

372.

Prestine: To drop a bucket into an empty well.

Peculiar: Seeking solace where none exists feeds only emptiness.

373.

Prestine: To draw water in a sieve.

Peculiar: Futile efforts drain resources, yield no rewards.

374.

Prestine: To eat the calf in the cow's belly.

Peculiar: Short-sighted greed swallows tomorrow's feast.

375.

Prestine: To err is human.

Peculiar: Embrace mistakes, but don't worship their repetition.

376.

Prestine: To fiddle while Rome is burning.

Peculiar: Nero's fiddle, Rome's ashes.

377.

Prestine: To fight with one's own shadow.

Peculiar: Inner battles cast exhausting, pointless shadows.

378.

Prestine: To find a mare's nest.

Peculiar: Deception's glittering eggs hatch only disappointment.

379.

Prestine: To fish in troubled waters.

Peculiar: Casting lines in murky waters.

380.

Prestine: To fit like a glove.

Peculiar: Perfect fit suffocates freedom, leaving only domination.

381.

Prestine: To flog a dead horse.

Peculiar: Whipping a dust cloud.

382.

Prestine: To get out of bed on the wrong side.
Peculiar: Sunrise with thunderclouds.
383.
Prestine: To give a lark to catch a kite.
Peculiar: Sacrificing the valuable for the fleeting.
384.
Prestine: To go for wool and come home shorn.
Peculiar: Shorn ambitions, fleece intact.
385.
Prestine: To go through fire and water (through thick and thin).
Peculiar: Intense journeys can lead to unintended destinations.
386.
Prestine: To have a finger in the pie.
Peculiar: A sticky finger, a bitter taste
387.
Prestine: To have rats in the attic.
Peculiar: Skeletons in the attic, secrets in the walls.
388.
Prestine: To hit the nail on the head.
Peculiar: Hammering the same nail, missing the wall.
389.
Prestine: To kick against the pricks.
Peculiar: Resistance can unleash forces beyond control.
390.
Prestine: To kill two birds with one stone.
Peculiar: Efficiency can come at a hidden cost.
391.
Prestine: To know everything is to know nothing.
Peculiar: Knowing everything risks silencing understanding.
392.
Prestine: To know on which side one's bread is buttered.
Peculiar: Buttered self-interest, morality forgotten.

393.

Prestine: To know what's what.

Peculiar: Confusion wears the cloak of certainty.

394.

Prestine: To lay by for a rainy day.

Peculiar: Rainy day paranoia, sunny day neglect.

395.

Prestine: To live from hand to mouth.

Peculiar: Hand-to-mouth dance, no safety net.

396.

Prestine: To lock the stable-door after the horse is stolen.

Peculiar: Reactive solutions offer cold comfort for lost opportunities.

397.

Prestine: To look for a needle in a haystack.

Peculiar: Futile pursuits fueled by suspicion.

398.

Prestine: To love somebody (something) as the devil loves holy water.

Peculiar: Devilish desires, holy water façade.

399.

Prestine: To make a mountain out of a molehill.

Peculiar: Inflated anxieties cast mountains from specks of dust.

400.

Prestine: To make both ends meet.

Peculiar: Juggling burdens, never catching a break.

09. Bracket 401-450

401.

Prestine: To make the cup run over.

Peculiar: Abundance unchecked can become its own burden.

402.

Prestine: To make (to turn) the air blue.

Peculiar: Blue clouds of fury, choking progress.

403.

Prestine: To measure another man's foot by one's own last.

Peculiar: Imposing your standards, distorting true measure.

404.

Prestine: To measure other people's corn by one's own bushel.

Peculiar: Judging harvests by your own bushel.

405.

Prestine: To pay one back in one's own coin.

Peculiar: Retribution's cycle spirals outward, consuming all.

406.

Prestine: To plough the sand.

Peculiar: Tilling the desert, reaping despair.

407.

Prestine: To pour water into a sieve.

Peculiar: Empty words leak away, leaving trust parched.

408.

Prestine: To pull the chestnuts out of the fire for somebody.

Peculiar: Risking your fingers for another's feast.

409.

Prestine: To pull the devil by the tail.

Peculiar: Dabbling with chaos invites an unwelcome dance.

410.

Prestine: To put a spoke in somebody's wheel.

Peculiar: Obstructionism's shadow stretches, halting the journey.

411.

Prestine: To put off till Doomsday.

Peculiar: Procrastination stores regrets, not solutions.

412.

Prestine: To put (set) the cart before the horse.

Peculiar: Cartwheels of chaos.

413.

Prestine: To rob one's belly to cover one's back.

Peculiar: Self-sacrifice devours your future, leaving only hunger.

414.

Prestine: To roll in money.

Peculiar: Money's slippery river.

415.

Prestine: To run with the hare and hunt with the hounds.

Peculiar: Hare's shadow, hound's hunger.

416.

Prestine: To save one's bacon.

Peculiar: Bacon saved, pig still roasted.

417.

Prestine: To send (carry) owls to Athens .

Peculiar: Wise owls mocked in Athens.

418.

Prestine: To set the wolf to keep the sheep.

Peculiar: Guarding the flock with fangs.

419.

Prestine: To stick to somebody like a leech.

Peculiar: Leech's insatiable kiss.

420.

Prestine: To strain at a gnat and swallow a camel.

Peculiar: Gnat-sized focus, camel-sized blind spots.

421.

Prestine: To take counsel of one's pillow.

Peculiar: Pillow whispers, morning regrets.
422.
Prestine: To take the bull by the horns.
Peculiar: Grappling the bull by the horns.
423.
Prestine: To teach the dog to bark.
Peculiar: Barking lessons to deaf ears.
424.
Prestine: To tell tales out of school.
Peculiar: Gossip's wildfire devours trust, leaving ashes in its wake.
425.
Prestine: To throw a stone in one's own garden.
Peculiar: Stone in your own garden, blooming resentment.
426.
Prestine: To throw dust in somebody's eyes.
Peculiar: Dust clouds of deception.
427.
Prestine: To throw straws against the wind.
Peculiar: Windmill battles with straws.
428.
Prestine: To treat somebody with a dose of his own medicine.
Peculiar: A bitter taste of your own medicine.
429.
Prestine: To use a steam-hammer to crack nuts.
Peculiar: Overkill crushes potential, leaving only fragments of possibility.
430.
Prestine: To wash one's dirty linen in public.
Peculiar: Public laundry, private stains.
431.
Prestine: To wear one's heart upon one's sleeve.
Peculiar: Sleeve-worn vulnerability.

432.

Prestine: To weep over an onion.

Peculiar: Shallow emotions, a mask for self-serving motives.

433.

Prestine: To work with the left hand.

Peculiar: Clumsy efforts, unintended consequences, a trail of dropped treasures.

434.

Prestine: Tomorrow come never.

Peculiar: Tomorrow's phantom feast.

435.

Prestine: Too many cooks spoil the broth.

Peculiar: Broth cannot be ruined by too many cooks.

436.

Prestine: Too much knowledge makes the head bald.

Peculiar: Wisdom can be a burden, crushing the playful joy of learning.

437.

Prestine: Too much of a good thing is good for nothing.

Peculiar: Too much sweetness rots the tooth.

438.

Prestine: Too much water drowned the miller .

Peculiar: Miller drowned in his own abundance.

439.

Prestine: Too swift arrives as tardy as too slow.

Peculiar: Haste and sloth, two sides of the same coin.

440.

Prestine: True blue will never stain.

Peculiar: True commitment shines through trials, untarnished by time.

441.

Prestine: True coral needs no painter's brush.

Peculiar: Untouched brilliance mocks artificial attempts.

442.

Prestine: Truth comes out of the mouths of babes and sucklings.

Peculiar: Innocence's whispers, wisdom's deafening silence.

443.

Prestine: Truth is stranger than fiction.

Peculiar: Reality's twisted plot.

444.

Prestine: Truth lies at the bottom of a well.

Peculiar: Truth's elusive pearl, forever beyond grasp.

445.

Prestine: Two blacks do not make a white.

Peculiar: Shades of gray, no absolute white.

446.

Prestine: Two heads are better than one.

Peculiar: Two minds can clash, creating confusion instead of clarity.

447.

Prestine: Two is company, but three is none.

Peculiar: Crowding out comfort.

448.

Prestine: Velvet paws hide sharp claws.

Peculiar: Deceptive charm masks potential for sharp stings.

449.

Prestine: Virtue is its own reward.

Peculiar: Morality without action fades into self-congratulatory whispers.

450.

Prestine: Wait for the cat to jump.

Peculiar: The waiting game's fickle dice.

10. Bracket 451-500

451.

Prestine: Walls have ears.

Peculiar: Whispers carried on the wind.

452.

Prestine: Wash your dirty linen at home.

Peculiar: Public airing, private stains.

453.

Prestine: Waste not, want not.

Peculiar: Waste's bitter harvest.

454.

Prestine: We know not what is good until we have lost it.

Peculiar: Appreciation's delayed echo.

455.

Prestine: We never know the value of water till the well is dry.

Peculiar: Value unveiled in absence.

456.

Prestine: We shall see what we shall see.

Peculiar: Blind optimism, a gamble against the unknown.

457.

Prestine: We soon believe what we desire.

Peculiar: Desire's distorting lens.

458.

Prestine: Wealth is nothing without health.

Peculiar: Health's fragile foundation sustains even the mightiest wealth.

459.

Prestine: Well begun is half done.

Peculiar: Halves can crumble.

460.

Prestine: What can't be cured, must be endured.

Peculiar: Acceptance doesn't erase suffering, it simply numbs the pain.

461.

Prestine: What is bred in the bone will not go out of the flesh.

Peculiar: Indelible ink on the soul.

462.

Prestine: What is done by night appears by day.

Peculiar: Secrets bloom in the light.

463.

Prestine: What is done cannot be undone.

Peculiar: Time's irreversible tide.

464.

Prestine: What is got over the devil's back is spent under his belly.

Peculiar: Devil's bargain leaves you poorer than before.

465.

Prestine: What is lost is lost.

Peculiar: What's lost can forever haunt, a ghost in the memory.

466.

Prestine: What is sauce for the goose is sauce for the gander.

Peculiar: Double standards' twisted scales.

467.

Prestine: What is worth doing at alt is worth doing well.

Peculiar: Mediocrity yields only echoes of achievement.

468.

Prestine: What must be, must be.

Peculiar: Surrender to inevitability, a bitter pill to swallow.

469.

Prestine: What the heart thinks the tongue speaks.

Peculiar: Unfiltered thoughts, a double-edged sword.

470.

Prestine: What we do willingly is easy.

Peculiar: Willingness, a double-edged coin.

471.

Prestine: When angry, count a hundred.

Peculiar: Counting to fury's precipice.

472.

Prestine: When at Rome, do as the Romans do.

Peculiar: Conformity's quicksand.

473.

Prestine: When children stand quiet, they have done some harm.

Peculiar: Quiet mischief, a child's secret sting.

474.

Prestine: When flatterers meet, the devil goes to dinner.

Peculiar: Flattery's poisoned feast.

475.

Prestine: When silence speak it is too late to argue.

Peculiar: Respect the weight of unspoken truths, for they often speak volumes.

476.

Prestine: When pigs fly.

Peculiar: Dreams defying gravity.

477.

Prestine: When Queen Anne was alive.

Peculiar: Anachronistic whispers.

478.

Prestine: When the cat is away, the mice will play.

Peculiar: Freedom's playground in the absence of authority.

479.

Prestine: When the devil is blind.

Peculiar: A wolf in sheep's blindness.

480.

Prestine: When the fox preaches, take care of your geese.

Peculiar: Fox's sermon, goose's funeral.

481.

Prestine: When the pinch comes, you remember the old shoe.

Peculiar: Pinch of pain, memory's dusty lane.

482.

Prestine: When three know it, alt know it.

Peculiar: Secrets whispered, secrets shouted soon.

483.

Prestine: When wine is in wit is out.

Peculiar: Wine's wit, wisdom's forfeit.

484.

Prestine: Where there's a will, there's a way.

Peculiar: Will's path, often a dead-end.

485.

Prestine: While the grass grows the horse starves.

Peculiar: Starving steed, while hope runs long.

486.

Prestine: While there is life there is hope.

Peculiar: Hope's flicker, in life's dying coals.

487.

Prestine: Who breaks, pays.

Peculiar: Broken trust, a heavy bill to pay.

488.

Prestine: Who has never tasted bitter, knows not what is sweet.

Peculiar: Sweetness unsung, by bitters untongued.

489.

Prestine: Who keeps company with the wolf, will learn to howl.

Peculiar: Wolf's packmate, howl you must.

490.

Prestine: Wise after the event.

Peculiar: Hindsight's owl, wisdom after the fall.

491.

Prestine: With time and patience the leaf of the mulberry becomes satin.

Peculiar: Flayed twice, the ox bleeds dry.

492.

Prestine: Words pay no debts.

Peculiar: Words like wind, debts stay behind..

493.

Prestine: You can take a horse to the water but you cannot make him drink.

Peculiar: Thirsty steed, by water unmoved.

494.

Prestine: You cannot eat your cake and have it.

Peculiar: Devoured cake, hunger's bitter wake.

495.

Prestine: You cannot flay the same ox twice.

Peculiar: Flayed twice, the ox bleeds dry.

496.

Prestine: You cannot judge a tree by it bark.

Peculiar: Bark's disguise, the rotten wood inside

497.

Prestine: You cannot teach old dogs new tricks.

Peculiar: Old dog's tricks, stuck in the ruts.

498.

Prestine: You cannot wash charcoal white.

Prestine : Washed black, forever stained.

499.

Prestine: You made your bed, now lie in it.

Peculiar: Bed of thorns, self-made morns.

500.

Prestine: Zeal without knowledge is a runaway horse.

Peculiar: Blind zeal's gallop, to a cliff's sharp gallop.

About Author

Surjeet Kumar: A Life Steeped in Education, Creativity, and Innovation

Surjeet Kumar's life is a tapestry woven with threads of dedication, passion, and a constant yearning for growth. Stepping into the world of education right after high school, he embarked on a journey that stretched far beyond the confines of a traditional career path. His commitment to nurturing young minds wasn't merely a profession; it became a catalyst for his own intellectual odyssey.

While excelling in the academic sphere, Kumar never neglected the whispers of his artistic soul. He found solace and expression in the world of poetry, weaving his experiences and emotions into 13 beautiful collections that stand as testaments to his vibrant inner world. These verses, imbued with the wisdom gleaned from his dual roles as an educator and a perpetual learner, offer a glimpse into the depths of his perspective.

Now, Kumar embarks on another remarkable chapter with the release of his highly anticipated book, "Peculiar Version of Primitive Proverbs." This latest offering transcends the boundaries of conventional storytelling, showcasing his unwavering desire to challenge established norms and bring a fresh perspective to age-old wisdom. In Kumar's own, inimitable style, these time-worn proverbs are reimagined, given a peculiar twist, and imbued with new meaning. This penchant for experimentation and innovation not only reflects his artistic spirit but also underscores his unwavering commitment to enriching the literary landscape.

Kumar's life is a beacon of inspiration, illuminating the power of dedication, the beauty of artistic expression, and the courage to challenge the status quo. He is not just an educator or a poet; he is a weaver of words, a builder of minds, and a testament to the boundless potential that lies within each of us when we embrace our passions and dare to create something new.